CARMAN PRESENTS

SATAN, Bite The Dust!

A Storybook for Kids

ALBURY PUBLISHING

All Bible verses are taken from *The Living Bible* (TLB) © 1971.
Used by permission of Tyndale House Publishers, Inc., Wheaton, Illinois 60189.

Carman Presents Satan, Bite The Dust!
A Storybook for Kids
ISBN 1-88008-934-3
Copyright © 1996 by Carman Ministries
P.O. Box 5093
Brentwood, TN 37024-5093

Published by ALBURY PUBLISHING
P.O. Box 470406
Tulsa, OK 74147-0406

An evil presence filled the air as Carman rode up to the saloon.

"Party's over!" Carman demanded. "Shut it down! I'm hunting for someone, y'all. He's a lying, thieving, rattlesnake, and he's broken every law. I've been sent with a warrant from the Body of Christ!"

Carman rested his hand on his gun and announced, "Every one of you unclean spirits, I'm runnin' you out of town! Depression, strife, disease and fear, your posse's goin' down!"

A demon growled from the bar, "Boy! The last tenderfoot who talked that, man, we sent him home in a box!"

Carman scanned the room. "But I know who I am through Jesus Christ. So I talk to you demons like dogs."

8

"You're hiding from the presence of God," protested Carman. "But I can feel your fear from here."

Suddenly, Satan appeared in the doorway and said, "You've rattled my chain, boy, long enough! You got somethin' in your craw?"

Then Carman said, "A praying church wants you to know..."

"Know what?"

Your kingdom's gonna fall!"

Satan
hissed...
"There's
gonna be
trouble
here
tonight..."

"You demons need to know I represent a whole new breed of Christian of today. I'm authorized and deputized to blow you clean away!"

"I've got a message to deliver from One who's true and just."

"We'll spit in your eye, you father of lies... Satan, **bite the dust!**"

Satan cackled, "Boy, you gonna take me on, and my unholy herd?"

 "Greater is He who's in me, than the snake I'm staring down!"

With the power of God's Word under his belt, Carman spoke with might, "Not only am I gonna take you on, but I'm gonna take you out by the Spirit and the Word! One by one you'll drop like flies, under foot and in the ground."

"You demon of alcoholism — you'll be the first to go! There is deliverance from you through Jesus Christ! So...hit the road!"

17

"You spirit of infirmity, you're not welcome here anymore!
I lay hands on the sick and they recover!

"You demon of false religion — you've preyed on minds so simple!"

"I bind the spirit of your songs! So — *EL KABONG* !!!
Play **THAT** in your temple!"

"Now Satan, you're next in line!
I'm gonna hit you where it hurts!"

"Cause I'm tired of **you** in my family..."

"...and I'm tired of **you** in my church!"

22

"I'm not my own!" Carman proclaimed.
"I'm bought with a price! I'm a Holy Ghost filled man!"

 "I'm tollin' the bell of your eternal destruction across the land!"

"And I'm authorized and deputized to blow you clean away!"

"I've got a weapon with two bullets that overcome all sin and crud!"

"One bullet is the **word of my testimony**..."

SATAN, BITE THE DUST!

The gun used
in this book
represents the
Word of God.

Guns are dangerous but
have no power
in the spirit realm.

"I use God's mighty
weapons,
not those made by men,
to knock down
the devil's strongholds."

2 Corinthians 10:4 (TLB)

The Word of God
in your heart and
spoken with the
power of Jesus Christ
breaks all demon power.

Satan, Bite The Dust! Bible Truths

Page 6

Carman could take on Satan's demons like he did on page 6 because of the authority Jesus gave His disciples in Luke 10:17-19. Listen to what His men said first, "...even the demons obey us when we use your name." Now listen to what Jesus told them! "I saw Satan falling from heaven as a flash of lightning! And I have given you authority over all the power of the Enemy, and to walk among serpents and scorpions [which Jesus referred to as demons], and to crush them. Nothing shall injure you!"

When we use Jesus' name and speak His Word, demons have to flee!

"And those who believe shall use my authority to cast out demons..." (Mark 16:17).

Pages 17 — 19

When Carman confronted Satan's demons on pages 17, 18, and 19, he knew that his fight wasn't with people. His fight was with evil spirits that don't have flesh and blood. The Bible says in Ephesians 6:12, "For we are not fighting against people made of flesh and blood, but against persons without bodies — the evil rulers of the unseen world...."

The Demon of Alcohol

The Bible calls *the demon of alcohol*, "drunkenness," in Galatians 5:21.

When Carman clobbered this demon on page 17, he knew that "...many evils lie along that path...." This is what the Bible says in Ephesians 5:18 about drinking alcohol. It invites this demon to enter into people's lives and leads to a horrible life of drunkenness.

The Spirit of Infirmity

When Carman knocked the *spirit of infirmity* out the door on page 18, he knew what Jesus said about healing the sick in Mark 16:18: "And they will be able to place their hands on the sick and heal them."

The *spirit of infirmity*, or "sickness," was removed from a woman by Jesus in Luke 13:10-13. Jesus laid His hands on this woman to heal her of her sickness.

The Demon of False Religion

The Bible warns us about the *demon of false religion* in 2 Peter 2:1, "...there will be false teachers among you. They will cleverly tell their lies about God, turning against even their Master who bought them; but theirs will be a swift and terrible end." Carman knew this when he commanded this demon to "go" and bound the spirit of its songs on pages 19 and 20.

The only way to tell false religion from the truth of Jesus Christ is to know the Bible's truth. Jesus said in John 14:6: "I am the Way — yes, and the Truth and the Life. No one can get to the Father except by means of me." So always read your Bible and you will know the *demon of false religion* if it ever comes around.

Finally, never forget that Carman was able to defeat Satan and his demons, just like you can, because of what the Bible says in 1 John 4:4: "Dear young friends, you belong to God and have already won your fight with those who are against Christ, because there is someone in your hearts who is stronger than any evil teacher in this wicked world." So always be confident in what Jesus says, and don't forget to tell *Satan, "Bite The Dust!"*

Additional copies of this book are available from your local bookstore.

ALBURY PUBLISHING
P.O. Box 470406, Tulsa, OK 74147